P9-AGM-373

66 × 6/24

Bumble and Bee

Let's Play Make BEE-lieve

ROSS BURACH

ACORN™
SCHOLASTIC INC.

To Max and Shaina — RB

Library of Congress Cataloging-in-Publication Data
Names: Burach, Ross, author, illustrator.
Title: Let's play make bee-lieve / by Ross Burach.
Description: First edition. | New York : Acorn/Scholastic Inc., 2020. |
Series: Bumble and Bee ; 2 | Audience: Ages 4-6. | Audience: Grades K-1. |
Summary: Bumble and Bee buzz around the pond, playing make believe, and trying to tempt Froggy to
participate in their games.
Identifiers: LCCN 2019044273 (print) | LCCN 2019044274 (ebook) | ISBN 9781338505252 (v. 2 ; paperback) |
ISBN 9781338505269 (v. 2 ; library binding) | ISBN 9781338505870 (v. 2 ; ebk)
Subjects: LCSH: Bumblebees–Juvenile fiction. | Bees–Juvenile fiction. | Frogs–Juvenile fiction. | Imagination–
Juvenile fiction. | Play–Juvenile fiction. | Humorous stories. | CYAC: Bumblebees–Fiction. | Bees–Fiction. |
Frogs–Fiction. | Imagination–Fiction. | Play–Fiction. | Humorous stories. | LCGFT: Humorous fiction. | Picture books.
Classification: LCC PZ7.1.B868 Le 2020 (print) | LCC PZ7.1.B868 (ebook) | DDC (E)–dc23

10 9 8 7 6 5 4 3 2 1   20 21 22 23 24
Printed in China   62
First edition, April 2020
Book design by Marijka Kostiw
Edited by Tracy Mack and Benjamin Gartenberg

Hive-Five!

Guess the Animal

4

8

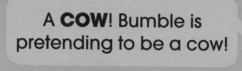

A **COW**! Bumble is pretending to be a cow!

Yes, Froggy! You are a **very** good guesser.

Will you play pretend with us?

Yes. I am **very** good at this game. Get ready to guess.

Woof! Woof! Woof!

hmmmm...

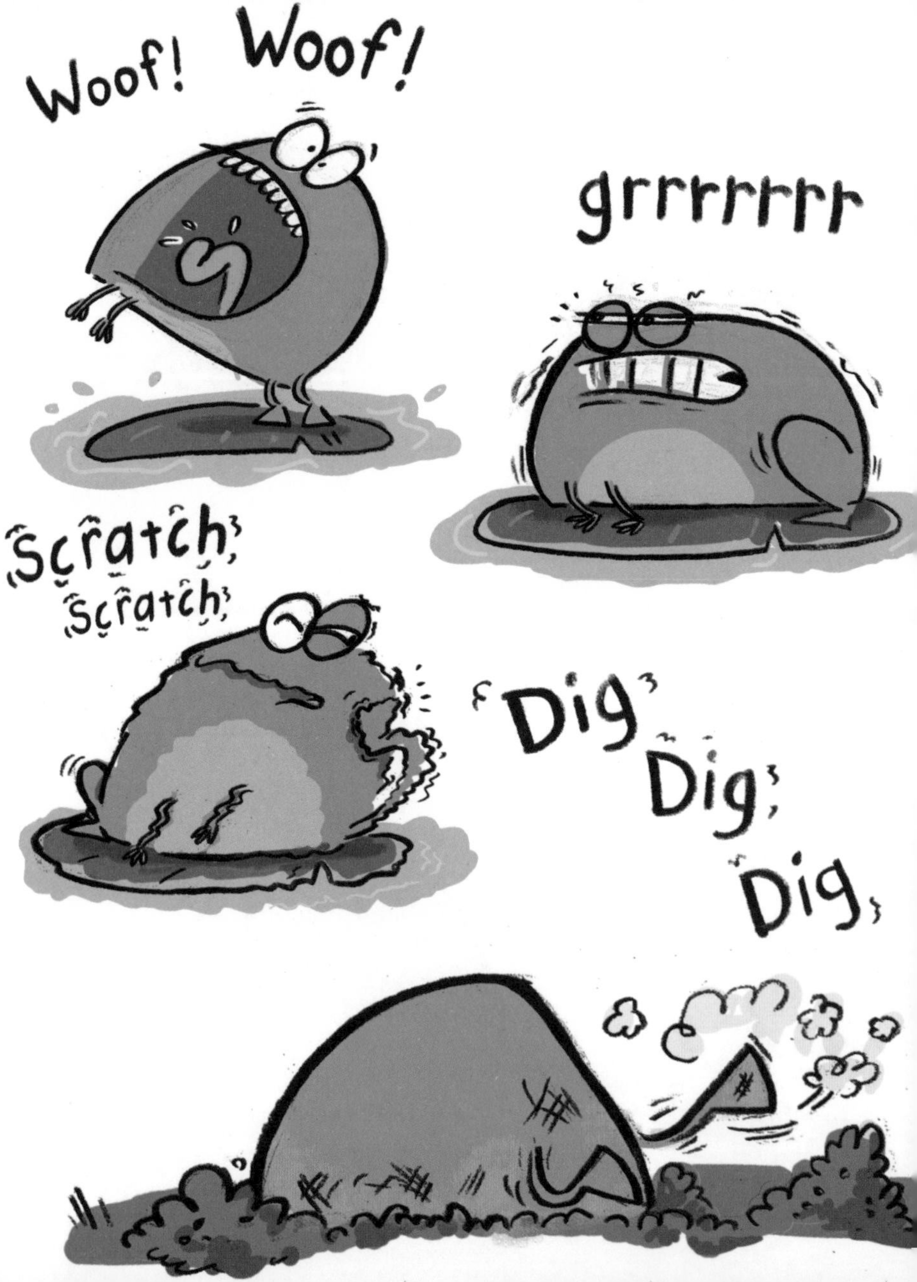
Woof! Woof!
grrrrrrrr
Scratch
scratch
Dig
Dig
Dig

(13)

Ahoy, Froggy!

And my name is **not** Bumble.

I am **Captain Bumble-Beard!**

And **this** is a treasure map. It will lead you to...

THE SWEETEST TREASURE IN THE WORLD!!!

I wonder what the **sweet** treasure is?

The sweetest treasure in the world!

For the record...
ice cream is also
a sweet treasure.

Hide-and-Seek!

Bumble!

Yes, Bee?

Want to play hide-and-seek with me?

Buzz-zoom!

41

About the Author

Ross Burach lives in Brooklyn, New York, where he spends his days drawing bees and frogs, and playing "guess the animal" with his family. He is the creator of the very funny picture books **The Very Impatient Caterpillar** and **Truck Full of Ducks**, as well as the board books **I Love My Tutu Too!**, **Potty All-Star**, and **Hi-Five Animals!**, named the best board book of the year by **Parents** magazine. Bumble and Bee is Ross's first early reader series.

YOU CAN DRAW BUMBLE!

1 To make Bumble's body, draw an oval. To make the eyes, draw two circles and two small dots inside.

2 To make the mouth, draw a closed semi-circle. Add a curved line for the tongue, and color in the rest.

3 To make the antennae, draw two lines with tiny ovals at the ends. To make the wings, draw two upside down U's with # signs inside.

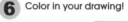

4 To make the arms, draw two sets of parallel lines. To make the fingers, draw four joined U's at the end of each arm.

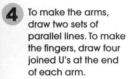

5 Draw two thick stripes across Bumble's body, and little lines for Bumble's fur. Add a thick line for the stinger, and four straight lines for legs.

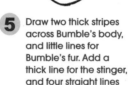

6 Color in your drawing!

Nice work.

WHAT'S YOUR STORY?

Bumble and Bee are playing hide-and-seek!
Do **you** have a favorite hiding spot?
What is your favorite game to play?
Who do you like to play with?
Write and draw your story!

scholastic.com/acorn